Art Direction by Paul Elliott
Digital Design by Rhion Magee with Karen Hoffman

Special thanks to Liz Keynes, Karey Kirkpatrick, and Clare Thalmann

Published by Dutton Children's Books,
a division of Penguin Putnam Books for Young Readers,
345 Hudson Street, New York, New York 10014

Printed in U.S.A.
ISBN 0-525-46420-4
First Edition
1 2 3 4 5 6 7 8 9 10

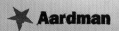

# CHICKEN RUN ™

Adapted by
**LAWRENCE DAVID**

Photography by
**TOM BARNES**

Screenplay by
**KAREY KIRKPATRICK**

Story by
**PETER LORD** & **NICK PARK**

Directed by
**PETER LORD** & **NICK PARK**

Produced by
**PETER LORD, DAVID SPROXTON** & **NICK PARK**

Tonight was the big escape. The prisoners hid in the shadow of their hut and listened for the guard dogs. Ginger, leader of the hens, clutched their secret weapon to her side, careful not to let the moonlight strike it and give away their position.

Yes, it was a dangerous flight for freedom, but for a flock of desperate chickens, the risk had to be taken. Ginger led her friends to the wire fence and took out the secret weapon. A soupspoon! She knelt by the fence, quickly dug a hole, and slipped through to the other side.

Next, Bunty, a hen gifted with the figure of a hippopotamus, squatted and pushed into the hole. She found her fluffles wedged between the fence and the ground. Frantically, she beat her wings and legs. "I'm stuck," she squawked.

Ginger grabbed Bunty's wings and tugged as the other chickens pushed from behind. Suddenly the beam of a flashlight hit Ginger. The farmer! The loud bark of his guard dogs filled the air. "Get back!" Ginger warned her friends. She pushed Bunty back into the yard and the chickens fled to their huts.

Before Ginger had a chance to get away, the dogs were upon her. Farmer Tweedy snatched Ginger up by her neck.

Wham!

*Thwunk!*

He tossed her into the coal bin and slammed the lid shut, leaving her in the dark. "Let that be a lesson to the lot of you!" he shouted. "No chicken escapes from Tweedy's Farm!"

To some chickens this would be a very scary spot to spend a night. However, Ginger braved it as she had so many other times when her escape plans had failed and she'd been caught. Coal wasn't that uncomfortable… and black feathers did bring out the green of her eyes. Ginger took out a Brussels sprout and bounced it against the wall as she dreamed up a new plan. There was no keeping this good hen down.

The next day Mr. Tweedy released Ginger and kicked her into the yard with the other chickens. "Company! Fall in!" crowed Fowler to the hens in a military chant. Being an old rooster on a chicken farm wasn't exactly the same as his former existence as a young rooster in the Royal Air Force, but Fowler took his work very seriously. He'd earned many medals in the RAF, and war or chicken farm, there'd be no slacking off on the regulations.

A bell rang and Mrs. Tweedy, the farmer's wife and the real voice of authority, stormed into the yard with her checklist. The chickens shuffled nervously as she walked down the line and stopped in front of one terrified chicken. "No eggs from this one today," Mrs. Tweedy sneered. She snapped her fingers, and Mr. Tweedy carried the chicken away.

Babs, a true featherbrain, kept on knitting as she always did. "Is Edwina off on holiday?" she asked.

Ginger shook her head. She knew Mr. Tweedy was taking Edwina to the chopping block. Chickens that didn't lay eggs for the Tweedys in the morning became dinner for the Tweedys at night.

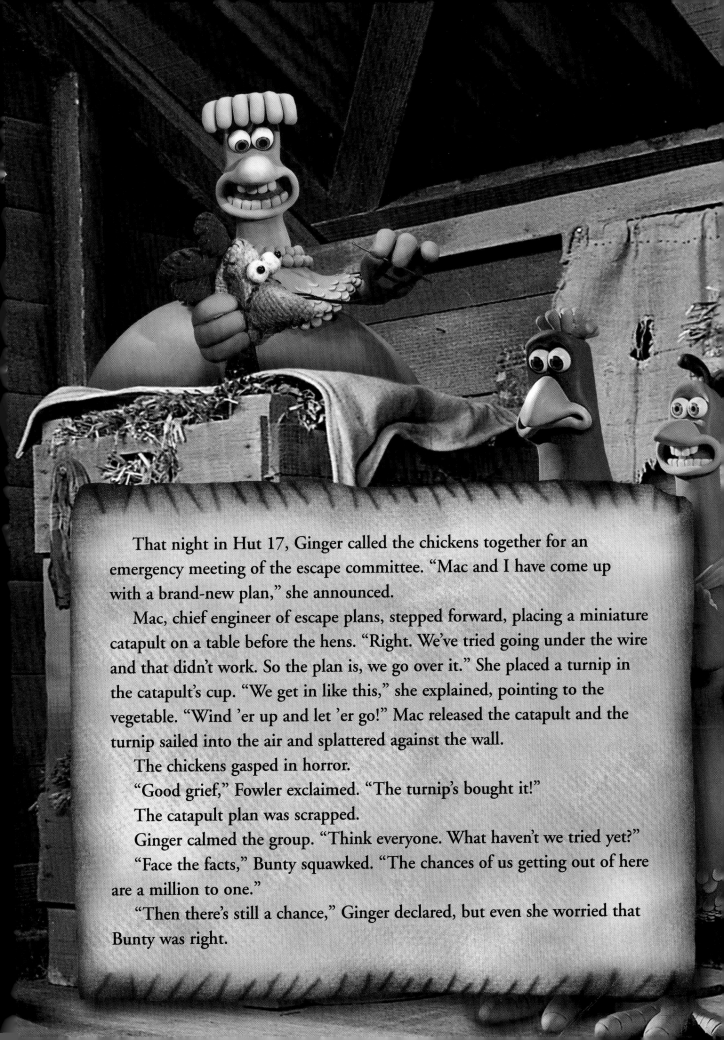

That night in Hut 17, Ginger called the chickens together for an emergency meeting of the escape committee. "Mac and I have come up with a brand-new plan," she announced.

Mac, chief engineer of escape plans, stepped forward, placing a miniature catapult on a table before the hens. "Right. We've tried going under the wire and that didn't work. So the plan is, we go over it." She placed a turnip in the catapult's cup. "We get in like this," she explained, pointing to the vegetable. "Wind 'er up and let 'er go!" Mac released the catapult and the turnip sailed into the air and splattered against the wall.

The chickens gasped in horror.

"Good grief," Fowler exclaimed. "The turnip's bought it!"

The catapult plan was scrapped.

Ginger calmed the group. "Think everyone. What haven't we tried yet?"

"Face the facts," Bunty squawked. "The chances of us getting out of here are a million to one."

"Then there's still a chance," Ginger declared, but even she worried that Bunty was right.

Ginger stepped into the yard. What was she to do? Her thoughts were soon interrupted by the arrival of Nick and Fetcher, two crafty farm rats and infamous scroungers. Nick snapped his briefcase stand open and pulled out a thimble. "How about this quality handcrafted tea set?" he suggested.

Fetcher plucked out a badminton shuttlecock and popped it on Ginger's head. "Or this beautiful number, all the rage in the fashionable chicken coops of Paris," he wheedled.

Ginger stared at the two rats, took off the "hat," and took out her list of escape equipment. "We need these things," she said firmly. The rats nodded, but they weren't going to work for chicken feed anymore. They wanted one and one thing only—eggs.

Ginger was horrified. "We can't give you our eggs; they're too valuable."

"And so are we," Nick replied. He picked up his briefcase and the two rats dashed away, leaving Ginger alone.

In frustration, Ginger banged the fence that surrounded the farm. "Heaven help us," she sighed. All of a sudden, the sky was lit with a flash of lightning followed by a loud thunderclap. And then, hurtling toward her out of the sky flew—a rooster!

"*Freeeedom!*" the rooster screamed. His wings flapped like sails. The rooster shot over Ginger's head and saluted before crashing into a weather vane, spinning around, bouncing off the power lines, and plummeting headfirst into the feeder bins.

At the sound of the crash, the other chickens rushed out of their huts just in time to see the rooster do a back flip out of the feeder, tipping it on its end. He stumbled, his head dizzy, and took a woozy bow. "Thank you, ladies and gentlemen," he crowed. "You've been a wonderful audience."

And with that, the feeder bin finally fell and knocked the rooster to the ground.

As chickens scurried over to see if he was okay a piece of poster drifted into Ginger's sight. She caught it. On the paper was a picture of the rooster flying through the air and the words "Rocky the Flying Rooster!" Ginger's prayers had been answered. A daredevil flying ace had come to their rescue!

"I carried you in!" Bunty boasted, giving Rocky a slap on the back that sent him reeling.

Ginger held up the torn poster. "Is this you?"

Rocky strutted around the hut. He loved to impress the ladies. "The name's Rocky. Rocky the Rhode Island Red. Rhodes for short. You know what they call me at home? The Lone Free-Ranger."

The chickens clucked, admiring the handsome rooster. Tail feathers like that didn't grow on pigeons!

Ginger nodded to herself. "A free chicken. I knew it was possible." She smiled at the flock. "We're all going to fly over that fence because Mr. Rhodes is going to show us how."

Rocky looked at Ginger as if she'd said pigs could fly. "Look, you're all swell chicks," he said, "but I'm a traveler. You hear that? That's the open road calling my name. Bye."

And with that, Rocky made a quick exit. He always left them wanting more.

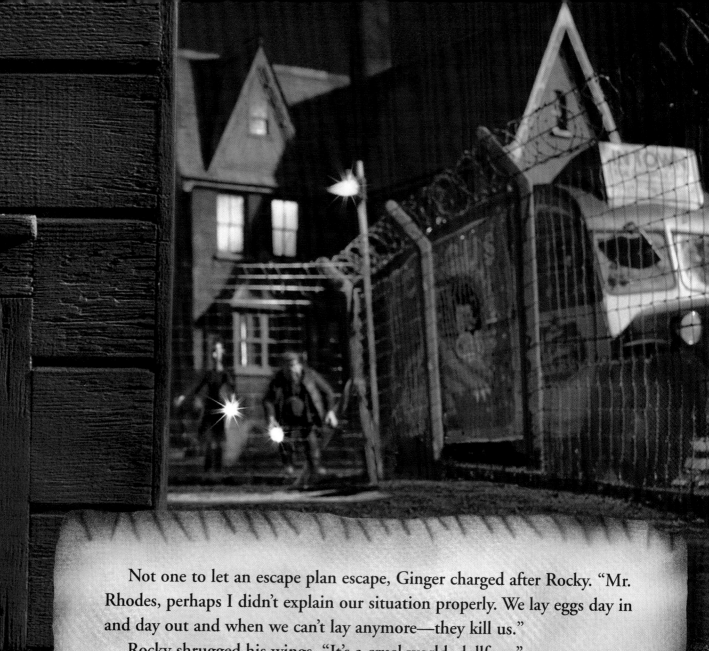

Not one to let an escape plan escape, Ginger charged after Rocky. "Mr. Rhodes, perhaps I didn't explain our situation properly. We lay eggs day in and day out and when we can't lay anymore—they kill us."

Rocky shrugged his wings. "It's a cruel world, dollface."

As Ginger pleaded for Rocky's help, a large circus van pulled up to the farmhouse. Rocky dove behind a hut. Ginger looked from the van to Rocky.

"You're on the run, aren't you?" Ginger asked. "I should turn you in right now."

Rocky gritted his teeth. "Now you listen here, sister," he said. "I'm not going back to that life. I'm a Lone Free-Ranger—emphasis on free."

"And that's what *we* want," Ginger reminded him. "Freedom. Teach us how to fly and we'll hide you." She held out her wing. "Do we have a deal?"

As the Tweedys and the circus owner began searching the yard, Rocky reluctantly shook Ginger's wing. "Time to make good on that deal, dollface."

Ginger clamped his beak shut and led him through a secret passage into Fowler's hut. "The name is Ginger!" she corrected.

Day after day Rocky kept the chickens busy doing push-ups and sit-ups, squat thrusts and jumping jacks. He told them to flap their wings to get their flying muscles working. He also suggested they build him a hot tub so his poor, sore wing could heal.

Fowler eagle-eyed Rocky as he instructed the hens. The old rooster didn't trust the fast-talking young cockerel.

Rocky watched the chickens flap their puny wings as a pair of hens massaged his shoulders. He had each chicken run up a ramp, flap her wings, and leap into the air. And each time, the chicken crashed to the ground with a thud.

Nick and Fetcher watched, laughing until their sides hurt.

Mac had been thinking about their flying plan and made a suggestion to Ginger and Rocky. "I went over my calculations and I figured the key element we're missing is thrust. Other birds like duck and geese—when they take off—that's what they have. Thrust."

The next day, with thrust in mind, Rocky had Bunty lie in a cart. The chickens pulled Bunty far back, using one of Mr. Tweedy's stretchy suspenders.

Nick and Fetcher sat in the bleachers and watched. "The tension's killing me," Nick gasped.

"It's gonna kill her." Fetcher laughed.

*Blam!* Bunty was released…face-first into the wire fence.

Nick and Fetcher hooted with laughter until Bunty bounced off the fence and soared right into the bleachers, sending the two rats scrambling.

The chickens saw Bunty's failed attempt to take flight and knew they were in trouble. No amount of thrust or flapping could lift these heavy birds off the ground.

That night Mrs. Tweedy calculated the money they were making from selling the chickens' eggs. "Stupid, worthless creatures. I'm sick and tired of making minuscule profits." She pushed the adding machine aside and glanced at an advertisement on the back of a magazine. *Tired of making minuscule profits?* the ad read. *Turn your chicken farm into a gold mine.*

Mr. Tweedy scratched his chin, thinking… "Those chickens are up to something," he whispered. "That ginger-colored one—I reckon she's their leader."

"Mr. Tweedy!" Mrs. Tweedy exclaimed. "I may have found a way to make us some real money around here and what are you carrying on about? Ridiculous notions of escaping chickens. They don't plot, they don't scheme, and they are NOT ORGANIZED!"

But Mrs. Tweedy did plot, did scheme, and was organized. She had a fiendish plan, and she reread the advertisement as she reached for the phone.

The chickens were feeling so low that Rocky hatched his own plan. He went to Nick and Fetcher and asked for a radio. In return, Rocky promised them every egg he laid this month. The greedy rats didn't know that roosters don't lay eggs, but Rocky felt his trickery was needed to cheer up the discouraged hens.

"We've been working too hard. It's time to shake those tail feathers!" he shouted.

Rocky turned on the music, kicked out his legs and danced to the beat. Babs, Bunty, and even old Fowler joined him, cutting a path across the floor. Mac did a little Scottish jig of her own. Feathers were flying, wings were flapping—the chicken coop was rocking.

Ginger watched, unsure of how dancing would help the chickens escape the farm. Of course, it did look like fun...and it was pretty swell of Rocky to go to all this trouble for the hens. So when Rocky pulled her onto the dance floor, Ginger couldn't resist the catchy beat. Rocky danced with Ginger, flapping his wings enthusiastically. He enjoyed seeing this pretty hen shake a leg or two.

Ginger smiled. "Your wing? It's better!" she said.

Rocky held up his wing. "Um, yeah... How about that?" he asked. Rocky stopped dancing and looked Ginger in the eyes. "Listen, um—there's something I've gotta tell you."

He was interrupted by the roar of a machine.

The chickens stopped their partying and rushed outside. The noise was coming from the barn, and billows of black smoke were flowing from the barn's chimney. The chickens stared, unaware that Mr. Tweedy had joined them. "I've got a score to settle with you," Mr. Tweedy said to Ginger. He grabbed her by the neck, lifted her off the ground, and carried her away as her friends watched in horror. He slammed the barn door shut.

The panicked chickens began to cluck.

"The enemy has taken a prisoner!" Fowler declared.

Rocky stepped into the yard. "What's going on?"

"They got Ginger, Mr. Rhodes," Babs wailed. "They're taking her to the chop!"

"For Pete's sake, fly over there and save her!" said Fowler, pointing to the open barn window, high above.

Quick as a flash, Rocky borrowed a hanger from Babs's knitting bag. He hooked it over the power line, grabbed ahold, and slid across the yard and through the barn window.

Down below Rocky a giant machine steamed and hissed and bubbled and smoked. Mrs. Tweedy smiled an evil grin as Mr. Tweedy strapped Ginger to the machine's conveyor belt. "Chickens go in. Pies come out," he said.

"Oh, great! Brilliant!" Ginger called just as she entered the pie machine. Her life flashed before her eyes: egg, chick, chicken—and now chicken pot pie...

From somewhere in the barn a voice called, "Hang in there! I'm coming."

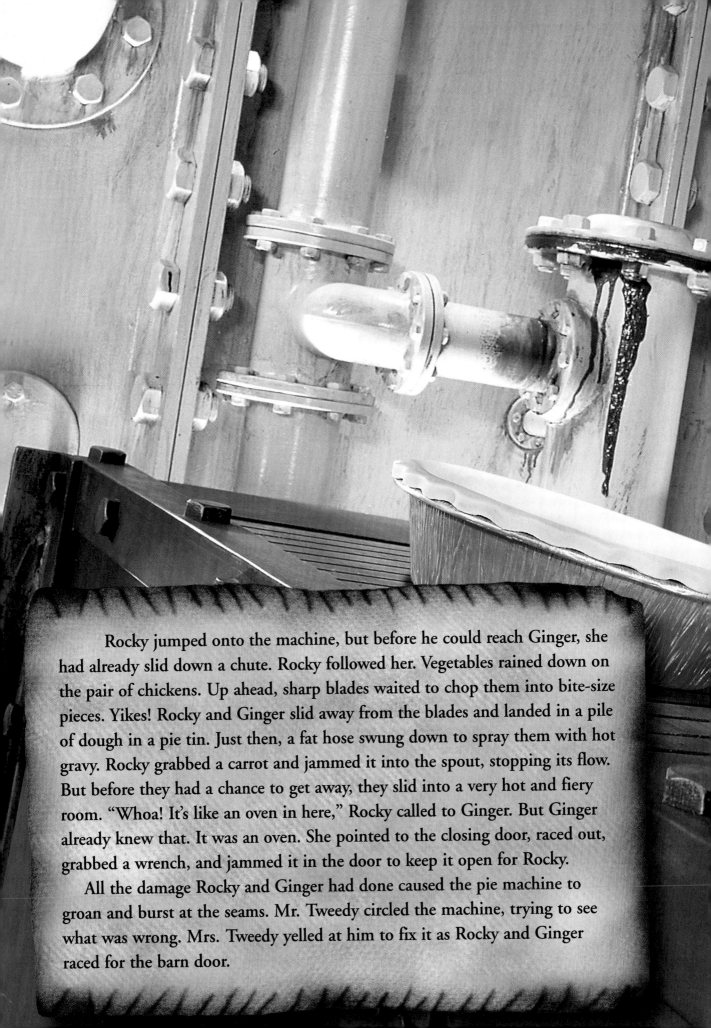

Rocky jumped onto the machine, but before he could reach Ginger, she had already slid down a chute. Rocky followed her. Vegetables rained down on the pair of chickens. Up ahead, sharp blades waited to chop them into bite-size pieces. Yikes! Rocky and Ginger slid away from the blades and landed in a pile of dough in a pie tin. Just then, a fat hose swung down to spray them with hot gravy. Rocky grabbed a carrot and jammed it into the spout, stopping its flow. But before they had a chance to get away, they slid into a very hot and fiery room. "Whoa! It's like an oven in here," Rocky called to Ginger. But Ginger already knew that. It was an oven. She pointed to the closing door, raced out, grabbed a wrench, and jammed it in the door to keep it open for Rocky.

All the damage Rocky and Ginger had done caused the pie machine to groan and burst at the seams. Mr. Tweedy circled the machine, trying to see what was wrong. Mrs. Tweedy yelled at him to fix it as Rocky and Ginger raced for the barn door.

Back in his hut, Fowler greeted the young rooster with a salute. "You have done a very brave and honorable deed, sir." He handed Rocky one of his war medals. "I await tomorrow's flying demonstration with great anticipation." Rocky looked down at the medal. They still thought he could teach them to fly. Feeling ashamed, he left the hut and climbed onto the roof to gaze across the landscape and wrestle with his thoughts.

A moment later, Ginger appeared beside him. She smiled at Rocky. "Thank you for saving my life," she said shyly. Was it the moonlight, or was Rocky really as handsome as a full feeder bin? Ginger looked out across the landscape. "I come up here every night, look out to that hill and imagine what it must be like on the other side. You know, I've never felt grass under my feet."

Rocky stared at Ginger nervously. The wind ruffled her feathers so delicately. "Yeah, well, um…as I've experienced it out there, lone free-ranging and stuff—it's full of disappointments."

"You mean grass isn't all it's cracked up to be?" Ginger asked.

Rocky gazed deep into Ginger's big green eyes. "What I'm trying to say is…" But he couldn't tell her his secret. "You're welcome."

Ginger smiled at her rescuer and their wings accidentally touched. She stood to leave. "Well…good night, Rocky."

"Good night, Ginger," he said as she left. She smiled. It was the first time he'd called her by name.

The next morning, Ginger went to Fowler's hut to fetch Rocky for the flying demonstration, but he wasn't there. All she found was the medal and the missing bottom half of the poster she had seen on Rocky's arrival. Now she knew his secret: the poster showed Rocky being shot out of a cannon. He couldn't really fly after all.

Out in the rain-drenched yard, Ginger nailed the poster to the side of a hut. The chickens gathered and gasped at what they saw. Fowler took the medal from Ginger, disappointed by the young rooster's desertion.

"Aye, a cannon will give you thrust," Mac said. "So what's the next plan?"

Ginger shrugged. "The only way out of here is wrapped in pastry."

Sad and frustrated, the chickens began squabbling, beating their feathers, and flinging mud at one another. Fowler stood in the middle of the fight and held his air force medal high. "No! A proper squadron must work together," he exclaimed, hoping to rally his troops. "That's why they give out medals!"

Bunty swatted the medal into the mud. "Will you shut up about your stupid bloomin' medals!"

But Ginger picked up the medal. "Fowler, what exactly is the RAF?"

The rooster puffed out his chest proudly. "The Royal Air Force is what."

Ginger flapped her wings, excited. "Everyone!" she yelled to the fighting chickens. "We're still going to fly out of here. Fowler's provided the answer."

They were going to build a flying machine.

While Mr. and Mrs. Tweedy were busy fixing the pie machine, Fowler retrieved old photos of the plane he'd flown in the RAF.

"Fowler will be the technical adviser," Ginger instructed. "Mac will handle the engineering. Babs—manufacturing. And Bunty, eggs."

"Eggs?" Bunty asked.

Nick and Fetcher approached the hens. If the chickens wanted the materials to build their flying machine, a trade would have to be made. Bunty handed an egg to Nick, and the two rats scurried off to bring the chickens what they needed. When they had supplies, the chickens formed an assembly line and nailed, screwed, hammered, and sawed to build their escape plane. Babs sat in a corner, stitching the plane's wings.

"Babs, great work!" Ginger told her.

"No problem, dollface," Babs joked.

In the barn Mr. Tweedy finished fixing the pie machine. He flipped the switch and the machine roared to life. Mrs. Tweedy smiled. "Get the chickens," she said.

"Which ones?" Mr. Tweedy asked.

"All of them," Mrs. Tweedy ordered.

Hearing the sounds of the pie machine coming back to life, the chickens knew the time had come to fly the coop. As they made their final preparations, Mr. Tweedy burst into the hut.

"Attack!" Ginger yelled. She immediately leaped onto Mr. Tweedy while another chicken shoved his cap into his mouth to stop him from screaming. The chickens tied his arms and legs with rope, then pushed him under the hut.

"This is it everyone!" Ginger called. "We're escaping!"

The chickens scampered around, pulling ropes and transforming the huts into a giant flying machine. Others rushed outside to set up a takeoff ramp and lay a string of Christmas lights across the yard for a runway. The chickens rushed to take their seats inside the makeshift airplane. Nick and Fetcher joined them. At Ginger's urging, Fowler took his place in the cockpit. "Cleared for takeoff," he announced. "Chocks away!"

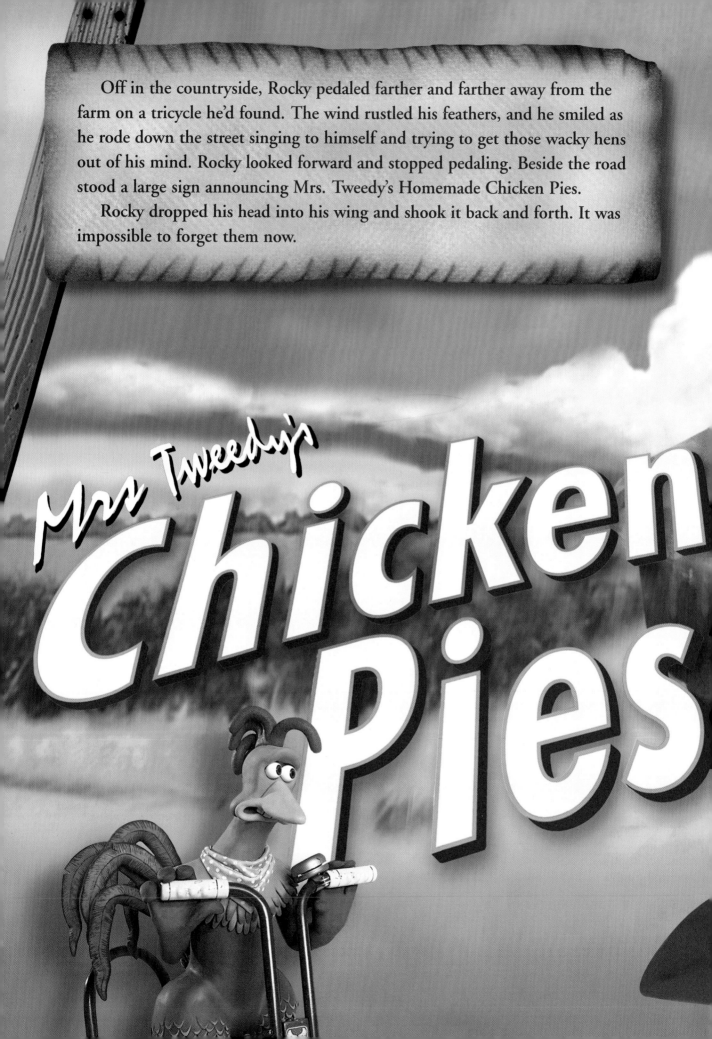

Off in the countryside, Rocky pedaled farther and farther away from the farm on a tricycle he'd found. The wind rustled his feathers, and he smiled as he rode down the street singing to himself and trying to get those wacky hens out of his mind. Rocky looked forward and stopped pedaling. Beside the road stood a large sign announcing Mrs. Tweedy's Homemade Chicken Pies.

Rocky dropped his head into his wing and shook it back and forth. It was impossible to forget them now.

*Mrs Tweedy's*
**Chicken Pies**

It's the WOMAN'S touch!

Back at the farm, the hens furiously pedaled as the giant flying machine began to roll down the runway. But before they reached the takeoff ramp, Mr. Tweedy escaped from under the hut and kicked the ramp on its side. Fowler swerved the flying machine and smacked into Mr. Tweedy, knocking him to the ground and tangling the Christmas lights around the plane's rear wheel. While Fowler worked to steer the plane in the right direction, Ginger dashed across the yard to right the ramp. As she struggled to set it up—*thwack*—Mrs. Tweedy appeared and swung her ax into the ramp.

Just then a loud cry filled the air. "Ginger!!!"

Ginger and Mrs. Tweedy stopped. It was Rocky, soaring over the barbed-wire fence. He crashed into Mrs. Tweedy, sending her to the ground.

He skidded the trike to a stop and flicked the bell on the handlebars. Success! Ginger beamed, but there was no time to chat. "Help me!" she cried. "The ramp!"

The two chickens heaved the ramp into place just as the plane rolled by them, up the ramp, and into the sky trailing the string of lights. Ginger and Rocky grabbed on and climbed up into the plane.

Aboard the plane, Ginger and Rocky stared lovingly into each other's eyes. Then—smack!—she slapped him. "That's for leaving," she said. "And this is for coming back." Just as she leaned in to kiss him, the plane suddenly jerked backward. They looked down. Mrs. Tweedy was climbing up the string of lights, swinging her ax.

"We need something to cut her loose!" Ginger called.

Babs quickly riffled through her knitting bag and came out with—scissors!

Rocky lowered Ginger to the string of lights. But Mrs. Tweedy's extra weight tipped the plane and Ginger slipped from Rocky's grasp. She managed to grab onto the lights, sliding down the wire until she hung just above Mrs. Tweedy.

Mrs. Tweedy swung her ax, but before she could hit Ginger, Rocky used Mac's catapult to fire eggs at her—splat! But Mrs. Tweedy would not give up. She swung the ax again and as it neared Ginger's head, Ginger got an idea. She lifted the wire and let the ax slice it right between her and Mrs. Tweedy. The cut string fell away, taking Mrs. Tweedy with it. She crash-landed right through the barn roof and into the chute of the pie machine!

KA-BOOM! The machine exploded, sending a huge cloud of gravy into the air. Mrs. Tweedy lay in a swamp of the brown ooze. Mr. Tweedy stood above her. "I told you they was organized," he said.

Ginger climbed back into the flying machine.
"Mission accomplished!" Fowler declared.
The chickens cheered and stopped pedaling.
The flying machine dipped.
"We're not there yet!" Fowler shouted.
"Keep pedaling!"
The chickens put their feet to the pedals and the plane rose higher in the sky and flew far, far away from Tweedy's Farm.

The chickens landed the flying machine and set up home deep in the countryside. No more roll calls, no more egg counts, no chicken-wire fences.

They had found a chicken paradise.

And Nick and Fetcher were deliriously happy to have more eggs than they'd ever imagined.

Rocky and Ginger stood side by side. Ginger looked down at the grass beneath her feet.

"Is it as good as you imagined?" Rocky asked.

"Better," Ginger answered, and grabbed his wing affectionately.

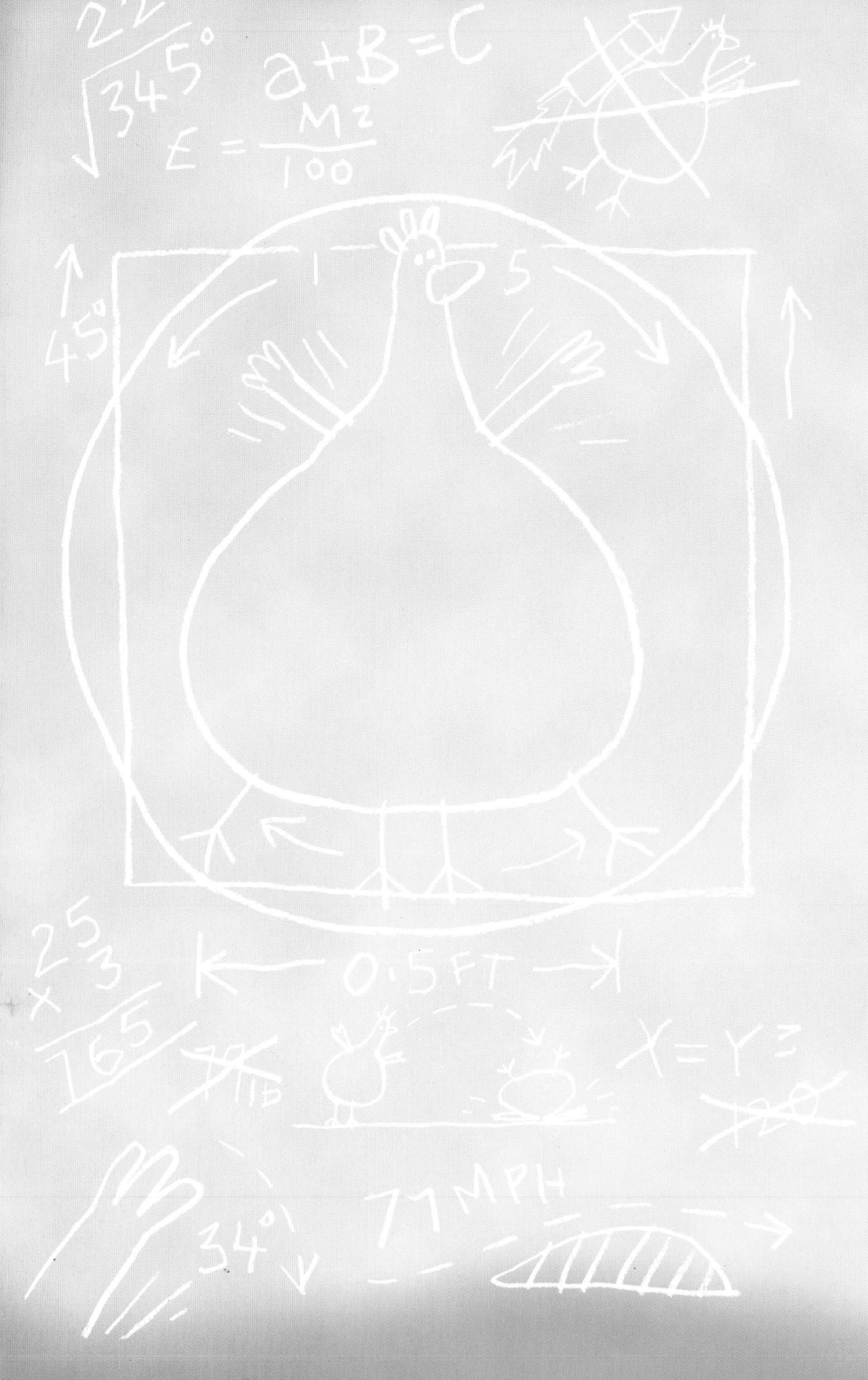

a+B=C
0.5FT
77MPH